Party
Mice

Written by
R. Wright and M. Butterfield
Illustrated by
J. Pickering and E. Corke

Monty, Milly and Maisy Mouse are feeling very excited. Today they are going to Cousin Michael Mouse's birthday party. They put on their smartest party clothes.

"Don't forget to take the present," says Mrs Mouse.

They are going to give Michael Mouse a bouncy blue ball as a present. Maisy wraps it up in pretty paper with a ribbon round it.

"I'm sure he'll like it," says Monty.

"I wish it was my birthday today. Then I would get presents," sighs Milly.

The three little mice set off for the party with
their friends the bluebirds. Monty isn't
looking where he is going.
He trips and drops the ball.
   "Catch it!" he squeaks, but it is too late.
The ball bounces off into the woods.

It bounces past Squirrel.

"Catch it, Squirrel!" squeak the mice. Squirrel tries to grab it, but she only gets the ribbon.

"Sorry I missed," she says, as the ball bounces off quickly through the trees.

The bluebirds fly after it, while the little mice
run behind as fast as they can. It bounces on
and on over the holes where the rabbits live.
"Catch it, rabbits!" squeak the mice.

The rabbits pop out of their holes and try to grab the ball, but they only get pieces of wrapping paper. The ball bounces over their heads and away into the bushes.

"Sorry we missed," they say.

The blue ball bounces down a path towards
Mr and Mrs Beetle, who are out for a walk.
   "Watch out," the mice squeak.
The beetles dive out of the way just in time
and the ball misses them by a whisker.

It bounces through a stream, where Frog is sitting quietly on a lily-pad.

"Catch it, Frog!" squeak the mice.
Frog tries, but it slips out of his wet hands and he falls into the water with a splash.

"I'm getting tired," cries Milly.

"Look at my smart clothes," cries Maisy. "Now they are all muddy and ripped."

"We'll have to go to the party without a present," sighs Monty unhappily.

They go sadly on to Cousin Michael Mouse's house.

"He will be very disappointed that we haven't brought a present," says Milly.

Michael's party is in his garden. Just as the mice arrive, the ball bounces over the hedge.

It bounces over the party tables – over the jelly and trifle, over the sandwiches and sausage rolls. On it goes, over cousins, aunts, uncles, grandads and grandmas.

Everyone tries to catch the blue ball.
  "This is the best party game ever," cries
Milly. In the end Cousin Michael Mouse
catches it. All the party guests cheer and shout:
  "Happy bouncy birthday!"